D1686701

Pit Bulls

Sarah Frank

Lerner Publications • Minneapolis

Copyright © 2020 by Lerner Publishing Group, Inc.

All rights reserved. International copyright secured. No part of this book may be reproduced, stored in a retrieval system, or transmitted in any form or by any means—electronic, mechanical, photocopying, recording, or otherwise—without the prior written permission of Lerner Publishing Group, Inc., except for the inclusion of brief quotations in an acknowledged review.

Lerner Publications Company
A division of Lerner Publishing Group, Inc.
241 First Avenue North
Minneapolis, MN 55401 USA

For reading levels and more information, look up this title at www.lernerbooks.com.

Library of Congress Cataloging-in-Publication Data

Names: Frank, Sarah, author.
Title: Pit bulls / Sarah Frank.
Description: Minneapolis : Lerner Publications, [2019] | Series: Lightning bolt books. who's a good dog? | Audience: Ages 6-9. | Audience: K to Grade 3. | Includes bibliographical references and index.
Identifiers: LCCN 2018035863 (print) | LCCN 2018037593 (ebook) | ISBN 9781541556652 (eb pdf) | ISBN 9781541555754 (lb : alk. paper)
Subjects: LCSH: Pit bull terriers—Juvenile literature. | Dogs—Juvenile literature.
Classification: LCC SF429.P58 (ebook) | LCC SF429.P58 F727 2019 (print) | DDC 636.755/9—dc23

LC record available at https://lccn.loc.gov/2018035863

Manufactured in the United States of America
1-46030-43353-10/30/2018

Table of Contents

Meet the Pit Bull — 4

A Dark Past — 8

The Right Fit? — 12

Coming Home — 16

Doggone Good Tips! — 20

Why Pit Bulls Are the Best — 21

Glossary — 22

Further Reading — 23

Index — 24

Meet the Pit Bull

Are you dreaming of a loyal dog? How about one that's both gentle and brave? Pit bulls are all of these things!

A pit bull isn't a single breed. It's a name for three different kinds of dogs. Staffordshire bull terriers, American Staffordshire terriers, and American pit bull terriers are all called pit bulls.

Staffordshire bull terrier

American pit bull terrier

American Staffordshire terrier

Early pit bulls were used for fighting. So some people think these dogs are fierce. But a well-trained pit bull is both sweet and smart. It makes a fabulous pet.

Most pit bull owners think their dogs are the best. And it's easy to see why. These dogs are hearty, good-natured, and really fun loving.

Aw, so sweet!

A Dark Past

The American Kennel Club (AKC) groups dogs by breed. Staffordshire bull terriers and American Staffordshire terriers are in the terrier group.

American pit bull terriers are not in an AKC group.

The AKC doesn't recognize American pit bull terriers. That's partly because pit bulls have a dark past.

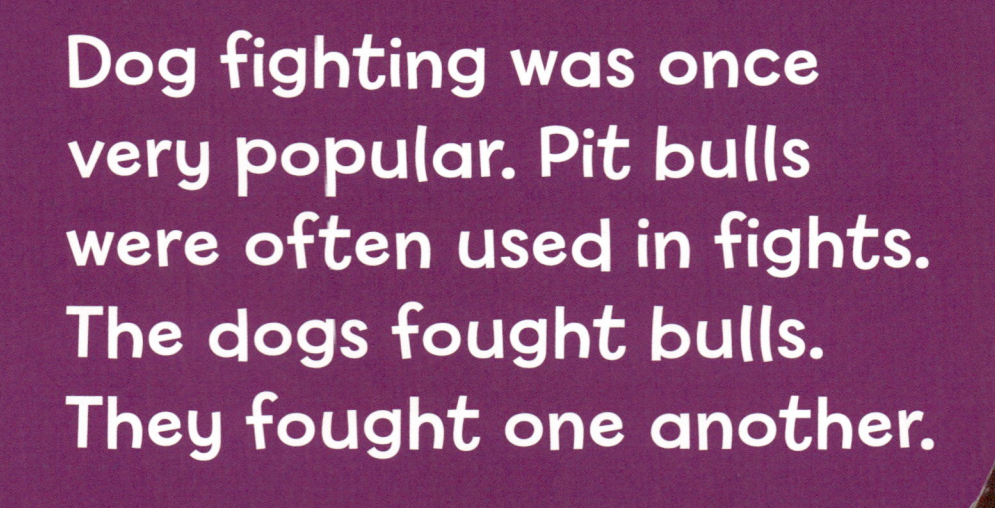

Dog fighting was once very popular. Pit bulls were often used in fights. The dogs fought bulls. They fought one another.

Bulls have very sharp horns.

The dogs got badly hurt. But people soon found better uses for pit bulls. The dogs guarded farm animals. **And they became very beloved pets.**

The Right Fit?

Pit bulls are special. But don't rush out to get a pit bull puppy. Talk with your family to see if a pit bull is perfect for you.

Does your city allow pit bulls?

Some cities don't allow pit bulls. That's because some people buy these dogs just because they're tough. They teach the dogs to fight even though they aren't supposed to.

"All dogs must be trained."

Do you have time to train your dog? Good training is important for pit bulls. Teach your dog not to jump up on people. Teach it to come when you call.

Are you up for a run?
Your pit bull will be! If you aren't into exercise, don't get a pit bull.

Whoa, doggy!

Coming Home

Did you decide you're a pit bull person? Then get ready to welcome your new friend home. Pick up some supplies, such as bowls and a leash.

Take your pit bull to a vet. The vet will examine your dog. Vets give dogs shots too.

Vets take good care of dogs.

Find out from your vet what food your dog should eat. And don't feed your dog table scraps. Birthday cake is for people, not dogs!

Keep your dog on a dog food diet.

If you treat your pit bull kindly, your dog will treat you kindly too. Show your pit bull lots of love. **You'll be rewarded with doggy kisses!**

Doggone Good Tips!

- What's a fabulous name for a pit bull? Here are some ideas: Jasper, Fido, Diana, Rocky, Jupiter, or Princess.

- All three pit bull breeds have tons of energy. Throw your dog a Frisbee. Take her for a nature hike. Pit bulls are always up for action!

- Give your pit bull lots of chew toys to play with. A bored pit bull is an unhappy pooch. It may chew on the curtains!

Why Pit Bulls Are the Best

- They are a dog of the rich and famous! The singer Pink, the actor Jamie Foxx, and comedian Jon Stewart have all owned pit bulls.

- Some are heroes. They work as search and rescue dogs. These brave pooches find and save people after disasters.

- They do well in the city or the country. In the country, they love to run in fenced-in yards. In the city, they'll relax in an apartment if their owners take them for long walks.

Glossary

American Kennel Club (AKC): an organization that groups dogs by breed

breed: a particular kind of dog

hearty: strong, healthy, and active

loyal: showing support for a person

terrier group: a group of dogs that tend to be feisty and have lots of energy

vet: a doctor who treats animals

Further Reading

American Kennel Club
https://www.akc.org

American Society for the Prevention of Cruelty to Animals
https://www.aspca.org

Bozzo, Linda. *I Like Pit Bulls!* New York: Enslow, 2017.

McKenzie, Precious. *Let's Hear It for Pit Bulls*. Vero Beach, FL: Rourke Educational Media, 2017.

Schuh, Mari. *The Supersmart Dog*. Minneapolis: Lerner Publications, 2019.

Index

American Kennel Club (AKC), 8–9
American pit bull terriers, 5, 9
American Staffordshire terriers, 5, 8

bowls, 16

food, 18

leash, 16

Staffordshire bull terriers, 5, 8

terrier group, 8

vet, 17–18

Photo Acknowledgments

Image credits: adogslifephoto/Getty Images, p. 2; Ivanova N/Shutterstock.com, p. 4; Erik Lam/Shutterstock.com, p. 5; Svetlanistaya/Shutterstock.com, p. 5; GPPets/Shutterstock.com, p. 5; Billy Gadbury/Shutterstock.com. p. 6; princessdlaf/Getty Images, p. 7; Grigorita Ko/Shutterstock.com, p. 8; Evdoha_spb/Shutterstock.com, p. 9; Vicki Smith/Getty Images, p. 10; Ariel Skelley/Getty Images, p. 11; JakubD/Shutterstock.com, p. 12; blutack/Shutterstock.com, p. 13; THEPALMER/Getty Images, p. 14; Aneta Jungerova/Shutterstock.com, p. 15; Bulltus_casso/Shutterstock.com, p. 16; Sonsedska Yuliia/Shutterstock.com, p. 17; sanjagrujic/Getty Images, p. 18; jenlinfieldphotography/Getty Images, p. 19; Eriklam/Getty Images, p. 23.

Cover Image: Eric Isselee/Shutterstock.com.

Main body text set in Billy Infant regular 28/36. Typeface provided by SparkType.